This book belongs to . . .

Copyright © 2019

mАke believe ideas ltd
The Wilderness, Berkhamsted, Hertfordshire, HP4 2AZ, UK.

www.makebelieveideas.com

Written by Rosie Greening.
Illustrated by James Dillon.

Every llama looks the same.
No one knows each other's name.
Say hello to Llama Joe.

Actually, that's Moe.

I'm JOE.

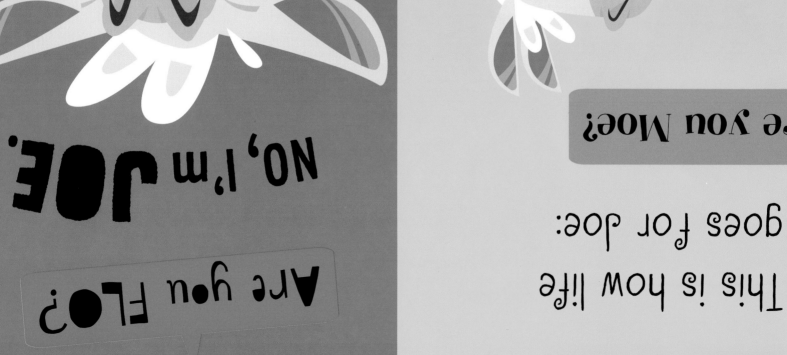

Are you FLO?

No, I'm JOE.

No, I'm JOE.

Are you Moe?

This is how life
goes for Joe:

I think I'm Joe.   No, you're Bo.

Am I though?

You might be Moe.   I don't know!

from the **HERD!**

It's time to **STAND OUT**

This is **ABSURD.**

I've had enough.

Slow down Joe, you're going to . . .

OK, FINE.
I take that back.

That's that.
I hate this hat.

I'm DONE!

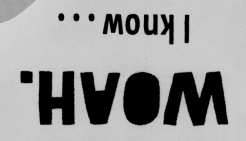

WOAH,
I know...

IDEA THREE

JOE

The HERD are in for such a shock.

Now this is how life
goes for Joe:

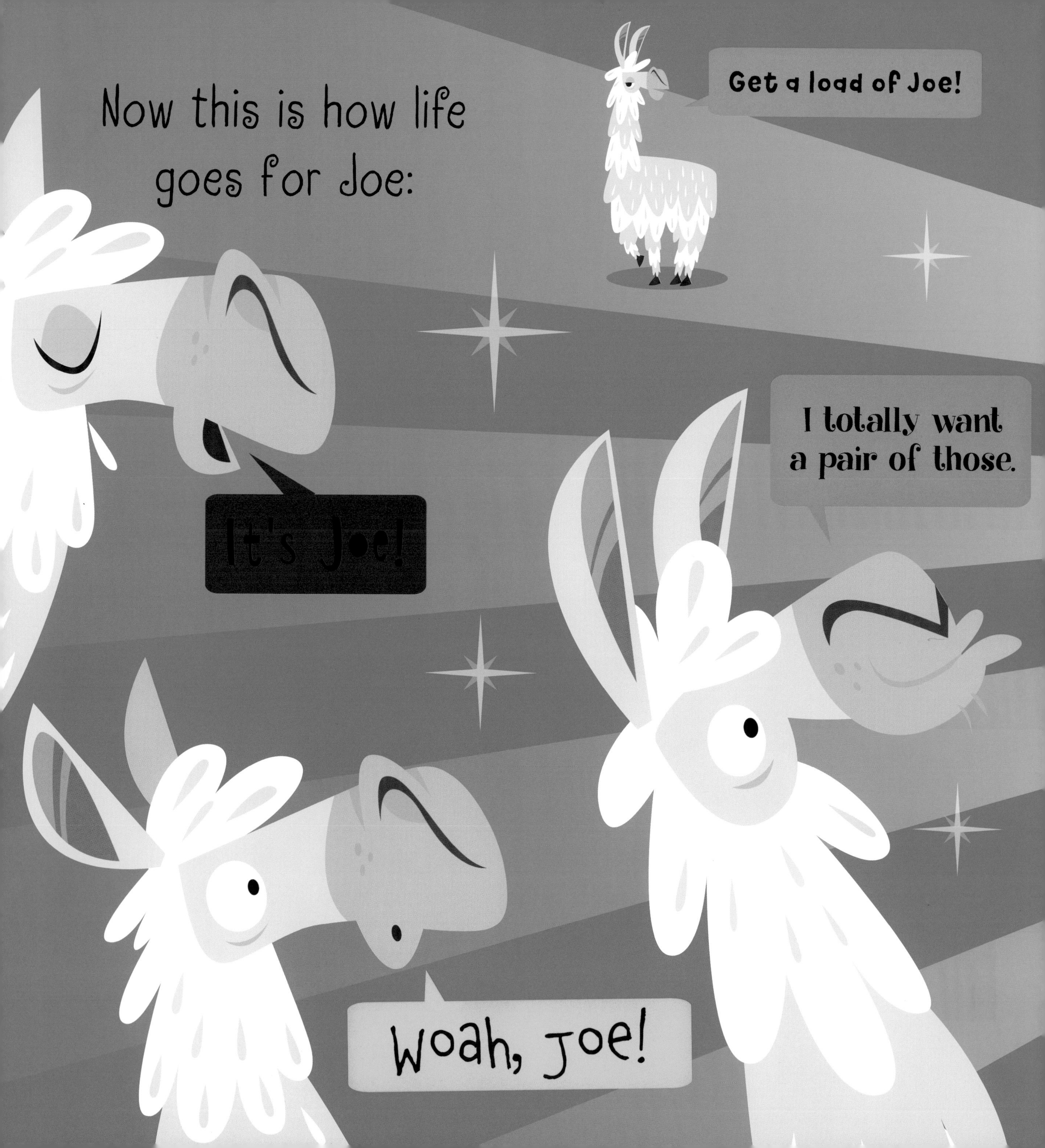

But soon, Joe gets
a nasty blow.

He wakes up, yawns,

. . . then

I'm JOE.

I thought I was Joe?

Hey, I'm Joe too!

for you... and you!

JOE

UNDERPANTS

But...
the REAL Joe knows
just what to do.

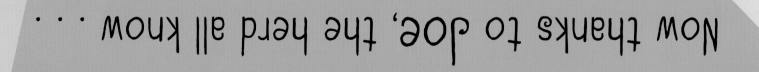
Now thanks to Joe, the herd all know . . .

... it's great to go AGAINST the FLOW!